Near Myths

Dug Up & Dusted Off

By Robert Kraus

VIKING

To Parker
— R. K.

VIKING
Published by the Penguin Group
Penguin Books USA Inc., 375 Hudson Street, New York, New York 10014, U.S.A.
Penguin Books Ltd, 27 Wrights Lane, London W8 5TZ, England
Penguin Books Australia Ltd, Ringwood, Victoria, Australia
Penguin Books Canada Ltd, 10 Alcorn Avenue, Toronto, Ontario, Canada M4V 3B2
Penguin Books (N.Z.) Ltd, 182-190 Wairau Road, Auckland 10, New Zealand

Penguin Books Ltd, Registered Offices: Harmondsworth, Middlesex, England

First published in 1996 by Viking, a division of Penguin Books USA Inc.

1 3 5 7 9 10 8 6 4 2

Copyright © Robert Kraus, 1996
All rights reserved

CIP DATA IS AVAILABLE UPON REQUEST FROM THE LIBRARY OF CONGRESS.

ISBN 0-670-85751-3

Manufactured in China
Set in Geometric

We know, we know!

The author, a master of the
Near Myth, uses Greek,
Roman, and Biblical names*
all together for the fun of it.

Don't look it up.

Laugh it up!

*Samson and Delilah

On top of Mount Olympus live the gods
and goddesses of mythology, and the
legendary heroes and kings of ancient times.
Mighty Zeus, greedy King Midas,
strong man Hercules, fiery Prometheus,
swift Mercury, and tuna-fish-salad-loving Neptune.
They are all here, plus many, many more.
A cast of thousands.
This is how their stories might be written . . .

MOUNT OLYMPUS

HELIUS

EUROPA

PAN

PROMETHEUS

THE BULL

MEDUSA

DIONYSIUS

ODYSSEUS

HERCULES WAS A NINETY-SEVEN POUND WEAKLING

Hercules was a ninety-seven pound weakling
who enjoyed lying on the beach
with his girlfriend Delilah.
One day that big bully Samson kicked sand
in Hercules' face, and ran off with Delilah.

Hercules joined a health club to get into shape.
Hercules worked out with dumbbells—and smart guys as well.

Before long he had iron arms, a glass chin,
buns of steel, and feet of clay.
He was a perfect specimen.

"Now I'll kick sand in that bully's face!" said Hercules.
He found Samson and Delilah lolling on the beach.
But Delilah had cut off Samson's hair
and turned him into a ninety-seven pound weakling!
"Why bother?" said Hercules.
So he kicked sand in Delilah's face instead.

"How rude," said Zeus, watching with
his telescope from Mount Olympus.
He hurled a thunderbolt at Hercules
to get his attention.

"You're bad, Hercules," he said,
"Picking on defenseless women."
"But . . . but . . . but," said Hercules.
"No ifs ands or buts," said Zeus.
"You must perform ten labors
to show your heart is in the right place.
These labors will go down in mythology
As 'The Labors of Hercules.'
You'll be famous!"

Hercules' first labor was to kill a lion
with his bare hands.
Then he had to kill a bear
with his lion hands!
"Isn't this cruelty to animals?"
asked Hercules.

In reply, Zeus tossed another thunderbolt.
The third labor was to pick
a peck of pickled peppers.
"No problem," said Hercules.

The fourth labor was to clean his room.
"That's a problem," said Hercules.
Then he carried the world on his shoulders,
for forty days and forty nights,
giving Atlas a much needed rest.
That was the fifth labor—whew!

The sixth labor
was to star in a movie
of his own life,
which wasn't easy,
as movies had not
been invented yet.

His last labor was
to clean the Aegean stables.
It counted as four labors
because it was such a big job.
He used soap and water,
and lots of elbow grease.

Hercules was really exhausted.
Then he went to bed and slept
for thirty days and thirty nights.
"It's okay to snore," said Zeus.
"You've earned it."

THE END

THE MADNESS OF KING MIDAS

King Midas was mad.
Not angry.
Nutty.

He made a muffler
from one of his wife's stockings.
It was called the Midas muffler,
and it would have made him famous.
But it wasn't enough.
He wished he had the golden touch,
and his wish was granted.

Everything he touched turned to gold.
His food.
His clothes.

His daughter!
"What a terrible mistake I've made," he cried.
"If only I could ungolden touch everything."
This wish was granted too.

He touched his food.
It became real.
He touched his clothes.
They became real.
He touched his daughter,
and she became real.

"Now, I'm exactly where I started," said the king.
"And I've wasted two wishes."
The gods decided to give King Midas one last wish.

For his last wish,
Midas again wished he had the golden touch.
"But this time, I'll be careful," he vowed,
scratching his nose.
King Midas immediately turned to gold!
His wife had him melted down,
and made into jewelry.

END OF MYTH

END OF KING MIDAS

MERCURY'S SANDALS

Mercury enjoyed horseback riding as a boy.
But when he got his
winged hat and sandals,
he stopped riding
and took up power walking.

Mercury's sandals and hat,
made him walk very fast.
"Slow down!" said his friend Apollo.
"You'll burn yourself out."
"Aren't you thinking
of Prometheus?" said Mercury.

And he wouldn't slow down.
And he couldn't slow down.
"What makes Mercury run?" asked Zeus.
"My sandals," said Mercury.
Suddenly he was flying!
"What fun!" he said.

Mercury flew higher and higher and higher,
until he took off for outer space.

After a year of flying around, he became tired

and started losing altitude.

Luckily Pegasus,
the winged horse,
was flying by.
And Mercury
was back in the saddle again.

P. S. Mercury invented sneakers with wings
and became rich and famous.

SO SING THE MUSES

PROMETHEUS WAS A FIREBUG

Prometheus liked to play with fire.
One day, he stole some fire from the gods,

and brought it down to earth.
The mortals were very happy.
Now they could have cookouts and barbecues,
and smoke cigarettes, pipes, and cigars.

The gods were very angry.
So they made cookouts and barbecues,
and cigarettes, pipes, and cigars
injurious to the health.

SO SING THE MUSES

KING NEPTUNE

King Neptune ruled his kingdom
under the sea.
His subjects were mostly fish
and the odd octopus.
But he didn't mind,
because he liked fish,
especially tuna fish salad.

For sport King Neptune drove his
four white horses across the ocean.
"Stop!" said the queen.
"You're making waves."
"That's the idea," said the king.

If you go down to the beach
on a moonlit night,
you will see
King Neptune in his chariot,
racing his four white horses,
with thundering hooves,
across the darkling waves
where the squid and
the tuna fish play.

SO SING THE MUSES